THE RUNAWAY PEA

WASHED AWAY

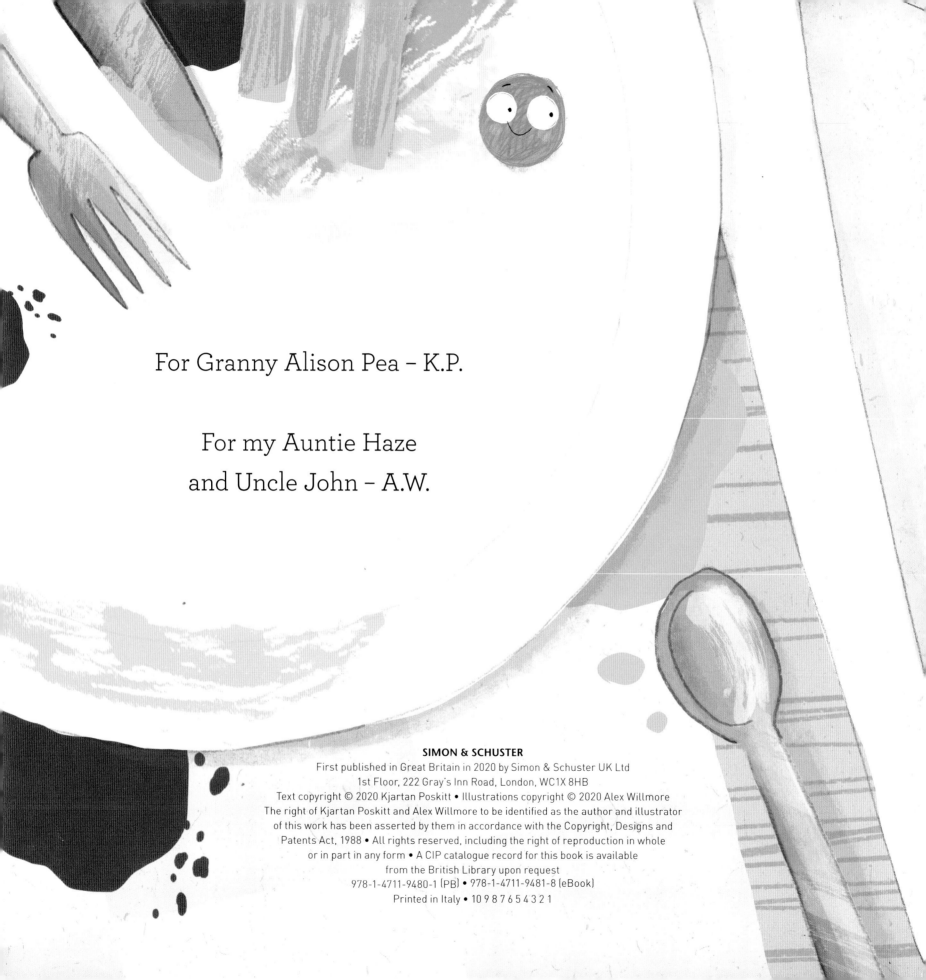

For Granny Alison Pea – K.P.

For my Auntie Haze
and Uncle John – A.W.

SIMON & SCHUSTER
First published in Great Britain in 2020 by Simon & Schuster UK Ltd
1st Floor, 222 Gray's Inn Road, London, WC1X 8HB
Text copyright © 2020 Kjartan Poskitt • Illustrations copyright © 2020 Alex Willmore
The right of Kjartan Poskitt and Alex Willmore to be identified as the author and illustrator
of this work has been asserted by them in accordance with the Copyright, Designs and
Patents Act, 1988 • All rights reserved, including the right of reproduction in whole
or in part in any form • A CIP catalogue record for this book is available
from the British Library upon request
978-1-4711-9480-1 (PB) • 978-1-4711-9481-8 (eBook)
Printed in Italy • 10 9 8 7 6 5 4 3 2 1

THE RUNAWAY PEA

WASHED AWAY

Kjartan Poskitt and Alex Willmore

SIMON & SCHUSTER
London New York Sydney Toronto New Delhi

The washing-up's finished,
so out comes the plug,

and the water goes
down with a **SWISH**
and a **GLUG!**

But under the bubbles,
what else do we see?
All on his own, it's a
washed-away pea!

TEA

Round and around the pea started to spin . . .
faster and faster then – **WHOOPS** – he fell in!

"Weee!" cheered the pea as he **SHOT** round the bend,

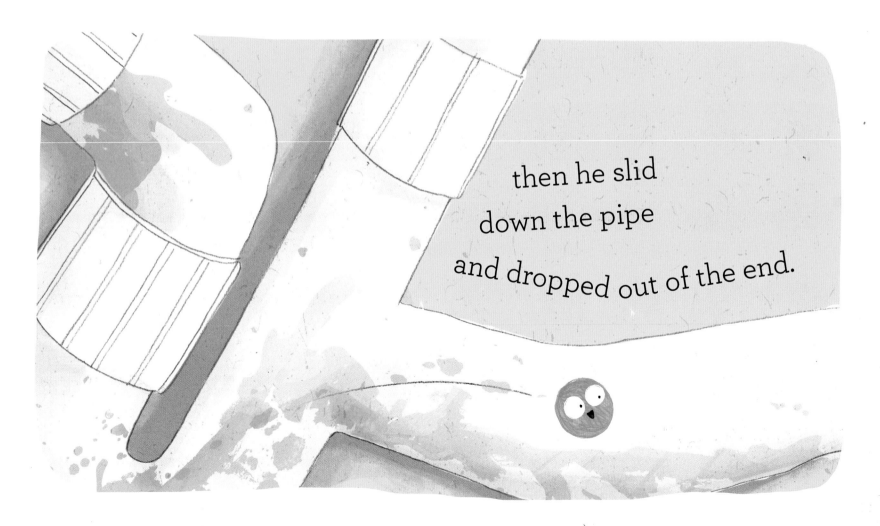

then he slid
down the pipe
and dropped out of the end.

Into the underground drain the pea fell –
it was cold, it was dark with a curious smell.

But did the pea mind all
the mess and the slime?

No, he was having a WONDERFUL time!

As he was drifting, enjoying the ride,
a cross little spider popped up at his side.

"Help me!" he shouted. "I need some dry land.
What use are eight legs when there's nowhere to stand?"

"Don't worry!" the pea said.
"Hold tight on to me.

We might just be small, but
we'll have fun, you'll see!"

But then came a

WHOOOSHHH!

which echoed like thunder,
and down crashed a big wave
which ducked them both under.

The little pea laughed as they tumbled about,
but the spider was shouting,
"We've got to get out!"

His eight little spider legs started to thrash
and sent them both over an overflow . . .

SPLASH!

"What a nice stream!" said the pea.
"We're in luck . . .

Let's stop for a rest and make friends with that duck."

But the spider said, "NO!
That's a big hungry QUACK!
She's after a little green circular snack."

The spider then paddled with all of his might,
into the reeds where they kept out of sight.

"Shhh!" begged the spider. "Keep perfectly still."
"You worry too much," said the pea. "You should chill."

Up came a fish from the darkness below.
"He's friendly!" the pea said. "He's saying hello."

But the spider said, "NO!
That's a big hungry eye.

If he says hello then
we're saying goodbye!"

He groaned as he paddled them out of the way.
"Oh dear!" said the pea. "Are you sure you're OK?"

"No!" said the spider. "I'm tired and sore.
And my legs are too wobbly to work any more."
"At least we're alone, so we're safe," the pea said.
Then suddenly . . .

...up popped a goggle-eyed head.

"A frog!" cried the spider. "He'll eat us for tea!
He'll gobble up YOU then he'll gobble up ME."

But the pea replied, "NO! Don't make such a fuss.
He's green just like me, so he'll never eat us.

He's come to be friendly,
we've nothing to fear.
Mr Frog, could you help
us to get out of here?"

The frog gave a nod and he then turned his back.
He flicked out his long legs, and gave a great

WHACK!

The pea and the spider went

PLIPPERTY

PLOP!

as they bounced on the water, unable to stop.

They finally rolled to a rest on dry land.
"Hooray!" said the spider. "At last I can stand.
Thank you so much for your help, Mr Pea!
The water is no place for spiders like me."

Then off ran the spider without a goodbye.
As the pea watched him go, he let out a sad sigh.

Tangled in cobweb and left on his own,
he felt rather helpless and lost and alone.

"What can I do?" the pea started to think,
when Boris the dog came along for a drink.

A loose bit of cobweb got caught in his hair . . .

and the pea found himself
swinging round in the air.

When Boris got home, it was time for his tea.
His eyes lit up and his tail waggled with glee.

SNAP!

went the cobweb,
the pea was sent flying!

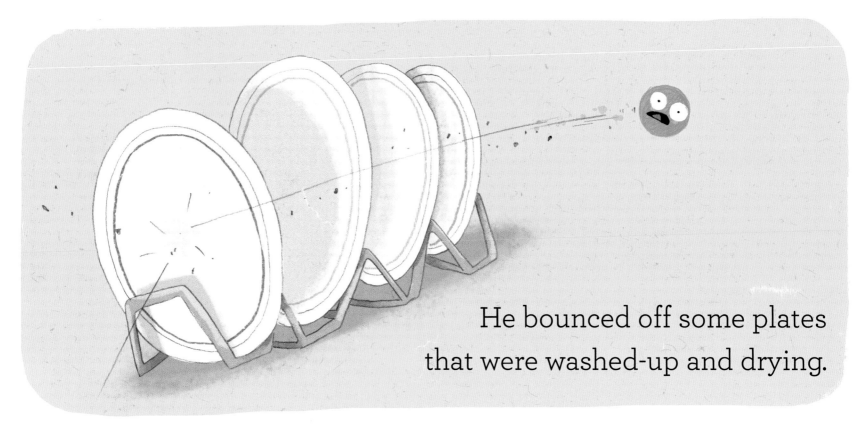

He bounced off some plates
that were washed-up and drying.

He pinged off the tap and . . .

he dinged off
the mop . . .

And finally into the sink he went . . .

PLOP!

But the washing was finished, and out came the plug, and the water went down with a SWISH

and a GLUG!

Round and around the pea started to spin . . . the pea started to spin then faster and faster then – WHOOPS – he fell in!

"WEEE"

He shot round the bend and down into the drain . . .

cheered the pea.

"It's all started AGAIN!"

THE END

(No peas were harmed in the making of this book.)